THUNDERBIRD

THUNDERBIRD

by Marilyn Sachs

with drawings by Jim Spence

A SKINNY BOOK

E. P. Dutton   New York

Library of Congress Cataloging in Publication Data

Sachs, Marilyn.
  Thunderbird.

  (A Skinny book)
  Summary: Dennis, whose main interests include
environmental protection and saving the world from
nuclear holocaust, meets a girl whose only passion
seems to be her 1957 Thunderbird car.
  [1. Friendship—Fiction. 2. Automobiles—Fiction]
I. Spence, Jim, ill. II. Title.
PZ7.S1187Th 1985 [Fic] 84-21252
ISBN 0-525-44163-8

Published in the United States by E. P. Dutton, Inc.,
2 Park Avenue, New York, N.Y. 10016

Published simultaneously in Canada by
Fitzhenry & Whiteside Limited, Toronto

Editor: Ann Durell   Designer: Riki Levinson

Printed in the U.S.A.   W   First Edition
10 9 8 7 6 5 4 3 2 1

for David, Melanie, Ryan,
Shauna, Shannon and Stacy Gin,
who love old cars

1

Monday
6:30 P.M.

"Could you help me, please?"

Dennis looked up from the desk. "Why, sure. What would you like?"

"The librarian upstairs told me I should come to the science room. She said I would find the book I want here."

"What book is it?"

"I have it written down. It's about the Thunderbird."

"I'm sorry," he said. "You have to go to the literature room."

"Oh, no." The girl made a face. "This is the first time I've ever been to the main library. It's so confusing! But I thought the librarian said I had to go to the science room."

1

"No," he said. "It's the literature room. That's where they have the books on Indian legends."

"I don't want a book on Indian legends. I want a book on the Thunderbird."

Dennis tried to speak slowly. He could see she was all mixed up. He could also see that she was very pretty and around his own age. "The literature room," he said carefully, "is where you find information on Thunderbird. I'd like to help you but . . ."

"Wait," she said. "Let me get this straight. I have to go to the Indian section to find a book on the Thunderbird?"

"Well, yes." He smiled. "Thunderbird was a god of the Southwest Indians, so . . ."

"Oh, no." She began smiling too. Her teeth were small and white. "I'm looking for the Thunderbird—the car."

"The what?"

"You know—the car."

"No," he said. "I don't know."

She was looking at him now as if he were crazy. Her teeth weren't so white after all.

"You mean you never heard of the Thunderbird?"

"No," he said. "I never did."

"But it's just about the greatest American car that was ever made."

"I'm not interested in cars," he told her.

She just looked at him with her mouth open.

"I never met anybody before who didn't know about the Thunderbird," she said finally.

She was wearing a funny shade of lipstick, he decided. In general, he didn't like girls who wore lipstick. He didn't approve of make-up.

"Can I help you?" he asked coldly, holding out his hand for the slip of paper.

"Oh, yes—sure—here it is. See, it's THE THUNDERBIRD STORY."

"I have to go into the stacks to get it."

"Can I go?"

"No," he said. "The public isn't allowed there."

She was waiting by the desk when he came back. She smiled when she saw the book in his hand.

"Oh," she said, "I'm so glad it's in. I can't wait to get it home and read it."

"It's a reference book," he told her. "You can't take it home."

"Oh, no!" she said.

"You have to read it here."

"But why? Why can't I take it home?"

"I don't make the rules," he said. "The book has an R on it. That means it's a reference book.

You can read it in the library, but you have to leave your library card with me."

"I have to go to work in ten minutes," she said.

"Do you want the book or not?" he asked. "There are other people waiting."

"Oh—well—okay—I'll take it."

"Your card please," he said coldly. He noticed that she had a large freckle on one side of her mouth.

2

Wednesday
6:09 P.M.

When Dennis came to work on Wednesday night, the girl was sitting at a table, reading. He noticed her as soon as he stepped into the room. It was probably that dumb book on that dumb car.

He pulled down the bottom of his tee shirt. It said NO NUKES.

Ken, one of the other pages, stood up at the call desk when he saw him. "It's a good thing you didn't come any later," he said. "Mrs. Douglas is having a fit."

"Well, she kept me ten minutes overtime on Monday," Dennis said. "She always keeps me late."

Ken made a face. "She's in a lousy mood tonight, so watch it."

5

"She's always in a lousy mood."

"Anyway, Dennis, I'm going. It's been kind of slow today. Maybe because it's raining."

Dennis frowned. "I like it better when it's busy. The time goes faster."

He settled himself down behind the desk and waited. The librarian, Mrs. Douglas, came out of her office with an angry look on her face.

"You're late again, Dennis," she said.

"No, I'm not, Mrs. Douglas," he told her. Very politely. "I punched in at exactly six o'clock. It took me a few minutes to get upstairs."

"You are supposed to be here, in the room, behind the desk, at six o'clock sharp. I've told you that many times."

"Well, I'm also supposed to leave here at nine o'clock," he said. Still politely. "And I didn't punch out until nine fifteen on Monday. I usually don't ever get out of here on time."

"Now look here, Dennis," Mrs. Douglas said, "you're a hard worker, and you have a good head on your shoulders. But it's not fair to the rest of the staff when you come late. Ken had to stay over ten minutes today. From now on, we'll have to dock you every time you come late."

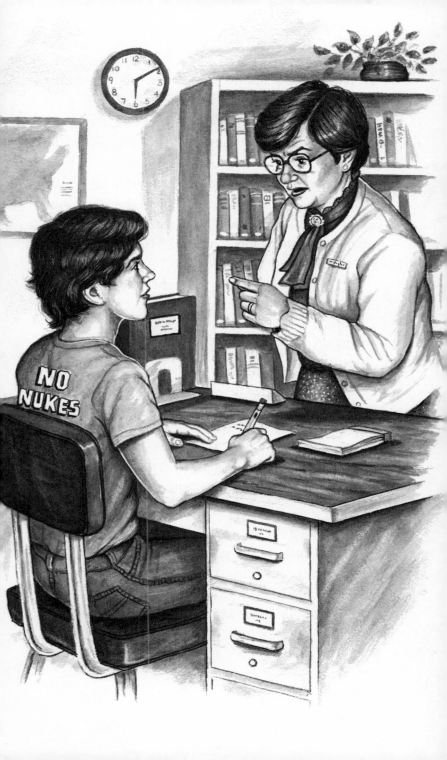

"Well, what about when I work overtime, Mrs. Douglas? What about that?"

"It hardly ever happens, and it's not the same thing. You are supposed to be in this room at six."

He wanted to argue, but she swept off.

A couple of people came up to the desk and asked him to get books for them. Then nothing much happened for a while. He watched the girl reading her book.

At seven o'clock, she brought the book back to the desk.

"Where's the other boy?" she asked.

"Which other boy?"

"The one who was here an hour ago. He got a book for me."

"He went home," Dennis told her. "Can I help you?"

"Oh, well—it's just that he told me his uncle had a 1963 Thunderbird. There's a picture here I wanted to show him."

"Oh!"

"He also told me his father used to have a Corvette and he hated it." The girl laughed. "It's a pretty crummy car. I pity anybody who has a Corvette."

She was looking at his shirt now, and he

waited for her to say something about it. But she didn't. She raised her eyes to his face.

"This is a wonderful book," she said. "I just wish I could take it home."

"Well, you can't," he said. "It's a reference book."

"I know." She sighed. "It's going to take me days and days to read it all. I'll have to keep coming back."

"Are you doing a report?" he asked. "For school?" He noticed that she had a very nice nose that turned up just a little at the tip.

She shook her head. "No." Then she giggled. "I own one."

"One what?"

"A Thunderbird. A 1957 Thunderbird. The best year of all. Here—I'll show you a picture of it."

She flipped through the pages and showed him a picture of a car.

"There—that's it—my car."

"Oh!"

"Isn't it gorgeous?"

He shrugged his shoulders. It was a car. An old car.

"That was the last year," she said. Her voice was hushed. "The last year they made a two-seater. After that, all the Thunderbirds were four-seaters. And they never were as good."

"Oh!" Dennis yawned.

"1955—that was the first year they made the Thunderbird." She had a faraway look in her eyes. "It was a match for any of those fancy foreign sports cars. I guess if you drove one you must have felt like a millionaire. That's what one of the ads said. 'What a mink coat does for a lady, a Thunderbird does for a male.'"

"That's disgusting," he said. "It's a stupid, disgusting ad. It's sexist, and it encourages women to wear fur coats. They're killing all the baby seals up in Canada to make fur coats. Don't you care about that?"

She didn't say anything. She opened her mouth, but nothing came out. He noticed her two front teeth were crooked.

"Here, do you want your card back?" He held out her card and took the book from her. She didn't even say thank you.

3

Friday
6:08 P.M.

"I want to talk to you," the girl said.

She was waiting for him by the call desk when he came to work.

"I came in yesterday," she said, "but you weren't here. There was a girl here, and she said you worked only Monday, Wednesday and Friday nights."

"I work Saturday afternoons too," he said, just to get the record straight. Today he was wearing his dead-birds tee shirt. It showed three dead birds and said STOP TOXIC WASTE.

Before the girl could say any more, Mrs. Douglas came rushing over to him.

"You're late again, Dennis," she said.

"I'm not, Mrs. Douglas," he said. "I punched

in at 5:58. But one of the guards asked me to help him move a table. . . ."

"I don't care what happened," she said. "You're going to be docked for fifteen minutes."

He started to tell her how unfair that was. But she just waved her hand at him and marched off. He said a few things under his breath about Mrs. Douglas.

The girl started talking again.

"You have some nerve," she said. "Acting like I was the one killing those little baby seals."

"I didn't say that," he said.

"Yes, you did. I would never kill a baby seal. I wouldn't kill anything. I don't even kill spiders."

"You said driving that car of yours was like wearing a mink coat."

"I did not. I just . . ."

A man came over to the desk and asked him to get a book on earthquakes. When Dennis brought it back, two girls were waiting. One wanted a book on horses. The other wanted a book on calories.

She was still there when he came back.

"I have to go in a few minutes," she said, speaking quickly. "I'm baby-sitting at seven, but

12

I wanted to say I think you had some nerve picking on me like that the other day. You made me so mad I couldn't even tell you off. That was the worst part. Not telling you off."

"Well, you were the one who said . . ."

"I did not!" Her cheeks were very, very pink. "I just told you what an ad said in 1955 when the Thunderbird was first made. I agree—it was a silly ad. Especially that part about women wearing fur coats and men driving the Thunderbird. I would never wear a fur coat. I love animals. I have a dog, and I used to have a hamster. I would never hurt animals."

"Driving around in big, gas-guzzling cars hurts animals," he told her. "Did you ever think of that? Did you ever think of all the wild animals killed on the highways? Or the way cars foul up the air? Lots of animals die from pollution. And people too."

"You must be crazy," the girl said. "I never met anybody like you."

"No," Dennis said, "I can believe it. You're probably too busy driving around in that dumb car of yours to meet anybody who's interested in animals or clean air."

Her cheeks grew so pink they were nearly purple. But before she could say anything, a boy

13

handed him a slip of paper for a book on reptiles.

She was waiting for him, standing on one leg when he returned.

"I've got to go," she said in a loud voice. "I'm late for my job. You just don't know anything. I don't drive around in a big car. I don't kill animals. And I don't make fun of people."

"You made fun of me," Dennis said.

"I never made fun of you."

"Yes, you did. You acted like I was a weirdo because I never heard of a Thunderbird car. I bet you never heard that Thunderbird was an Indian god! I didn't make fun of you because you didn't know that."

The girl looked at the clock and moaned. "I've got to go. I've got to go. You're crazy, but I have to go."

She put the book on his desk. He handed back her library card. He noticed her name was Tina Sabella.

"I'll be back Monday," she said in an unpleasant voice. "I'll tell you what I think of you then."

"I can hardly wait," he told her.

4

Monday
6:06 P.M.

He was out of breath when he reached the desk on Monday. Nobody was sitting there. Mrs. Douglas wasn't in sight either. He sat down and began shuffling through some of the papers. If she came out of the office and saw him, she might think he had been sitting there for six minutes.

After a while, he looked around the room for the girl. He had been thinking about her all weekend. She wasn't anywhere in sight. He felt disappointed.

Mrs. Douglas came out of her office at 6:43. She told him she was docking him another fifteen minutes. She also said he would be docked a half hour unless he came in on time.

It was a lousy evening. He was wearing his NO NUKES tee shirt, and it smelled sweaty by the time the library closed.

The girl, Tina Sabella, never showed up.

5

"Congratulations, Dennis," said Mrs. Douglas. "You're three minutes early. I knew you could do it."

He pulled at the bottom of his new tee shirt. It said NO ACID RAIN and showed a dead tree.

"It's been a very slow day," she said. "I suppose because tomorrow is Thanksgiving. I can hardly wait. It really is my favorite holiday."

"It's not mine," he said. "And I guess it isn't for the turkeys either."

"Oh, that's right," she said. "I forgot that you're a vegetarian."

Tina was standing by the desk.

18

"Listen," she said. "I want to tell you something."

"Oh," he said, "it's you."

"I probably shouldn't even bother speaking to you, but I decided I needed to get a few things off my chest."

He had a bunch of nasty digs ready for her too, but she was wearing a blue sweater that looked nice. Blue was his favorite color.

She looked at his tee shirt and began shaking her head. "Are you always against everything?" she asked. "Aren't you ever FOR something?"

"What do you mean?"

"Just look at your tee shirt. It says No Acid Rain. Last Friday, you were wearing a tee shirt that said No Toxic Waste. On another day, you had one that said Stop the Nukes."

"No," he interrupted. "The one I wore on Friday said Stop Toxic Waste, and the other one said No Nukes."

"Anyway," Tina continued, "you're always against something. Against cars too. Isn't there anything you're for?"

"Lots of things I'm for," Dennis said. "I'm president of a hiking club at school, and I belong to Greenpeace. I'm for fresh air and animals and peace."

"So why are you always so angry?"

"I'm not angry," he said.

"Yes, you are. You're angry at me, and I never even did anything to you. I never made fun of you either, and I do so know that Thunderbird was the name of an Indian god."

"You do?"

"Sure I do. See, it says so, right here in the book. It says Thunderbird meant good luck to the Indians. They believed that nobody could see Thunderbird, except in flashes, because it flew so quickly through the clouds."

"But you didn't know it was the name of an Indian god until you read it in the book," he insisted.

"That's right," she admitted. "But I know now." She smiled at him. "Thunderbird is such a beautiful name for a car. The book says they had a bunch of other names they considered, like Bronco or Cobra or Wasp. I don't think it would be as wonderful with another name."

"Why not?" he asked. "Didn't you ever hear 'A rose by any other name would smell as sweet'?"

"No," she said. "I never heard that."

"Well, anyway," he said. "What did you want to tell me? You said you wanted to tell me something."

"That's right. Okay. You know how you said all I do is drive around in my Thunderbird?"

"Yes," he said. "I remember."

"Well, it's not true. I can't drive around in it."

"Why not?" he asked. "Is it because your father won't let you?"

"What's it got to do with my father?"

"Isn't it his car?"

"No," she said. "My father has a Rabbit."

"A live one?"

"Are you kidding?"

"You said it," Dennis told her. "You said your father had a rabbit."

"Okay, okay," she said, taking a deep breath and speaking very slowly. "I mean he has a Rabbit car—you know—Volkswagen puts out a car called the Rabbit."

He didn't know, but he wasn't going to admit it. He decided the color of her sweater wasn't such a great blue after all.

"Never mind," she said. "There is a car called the Rabbit, and my father has a Rabbit. It's one of those little foreign cars that chugs along and can hardly make it up a hill. It has one of those four-cylinder engines. It's like a toy."

"So who has the Thunderbird?" he asked.

"I do. It's mine. A 1957 Thunderbird. I bought it."

"I guess it must have been pretty cheap," he said, "since it's such an old car."

"Do you know what a 1957 Thunderbird would cost if it was in good shape?" she asked.

"No. What?"

"Over twenty-five thousand dollars," she told him. "It's a collector's item. An American classic. Here, I'll show you a picture of one."

"You showed me one already," he said quickly. "You must have a lot of money if you can afford one."

"No," she said. "I had seven hundred dollars saved up. My father said when I had a thousand he would help me pick out an old car. He wanted me to buy a little car. Like a Volkswagen or a Honda. One of those little foreign cars. He said he would help me work on it."

"So you bought a Thunderbird instead?"

"Yes." She smiled at him. Her sweater really was a pretty blue. "But I have to tell you something. It doesn't go."

"What do you mean it doesn't go?"

"I saw it on the street one day, on my way home from school," she said. "It's a funny thing but I never go home that way. Just on this one day I did. It must have been fate or something. But I saw it that day. Two little kids were sitting on it. One of them said his brother owned it and was going to junk it because it didn't go. I asked him if his brother was home, and he said yes. So I went and talked to him and I bought it."

"You mean," Dennis said, "you bought a car that doesn't go?"

"Oh, yes," she said. "I got it for only six hundred dollars. I could get more than that just for the parts. The parts are beautiful. The hubcaps have a feather design, and even the bumpers are gorgeous. I know somebody who paid fifty dollars just for the original cigarette lighter."

"And you said I was crazy?"

"It was just sitting out there on the street," she said, not hearing him. "With those two kids jumping up and down on it. Somebody had painted it an ugly yellow, and the grille was smashed in. The right fender was dented, and so was the door. The glass was out of both porthole windows, and there was rust all over the body."

"You threw away six hundred dollars on a car that doesn't go?" Dennis said. "I can't believe it."

"I knew what it would look like when I finished fixing it up," Tina said. "I could see it in my mind all shiny and red with the grille straightened out and the glass back in the porthole windows. I could see it the way the Indians saw Thunderbird—whizzing down the road with me in it. Going so fast hardly anybody could see us. I could feel the wheel under my hands and see the road smoking behind me."

It was a good thing Mrs. Douglas came over to tell him to straighten up some of the magazines or he might have said something nasty. He didn't want to say anything nasty, but she certainly was one crazy girl.

6

Saturday
1:07 P.M.

"How did you enjoy Thanksgiving?"

"Oh, Tina!" Dennis saw Mrs. Douglas shaking her head as he slid behind the call desk. It wasn't his fault he was late. He had to wait nearly twenty minutes for the number 2 bus. Maybe because it was the holiday weekend, the buses were even later than usual. He hated holidays—especially Thanksgiving.

Tina looked at his tee shirt. This one just said GREENPEACE."

"What does it mean?" she said. "Greenpeace?"

Mrs. Douglas had seemed to be on her way over to him, but somebody stopped her to ask a question. Maybe it would be a real tough

27

question, and she would forget about him.

"Which one do you want me to answer first?" he said. He noticed that Tina was holding the Thunderbird book. Probably she had spent the whole morning reading it. What a waste!

"What do you mean?"

"First you asked me if I enjoyed Thanksgiving and then, before I answered, you asked me what Greenpeace meant. Which question do you want me to answer first?"

"Boy," she said, "you sure are a crank!" But she was smiling.

"I didn't enjoy Thanksgiving," he said, "because I'm a vegetarian. I don't like thinking about all those turkeys. Greenpeace is an organization set up to protect wild creatures from being killed off—like the whales and the baby seals."

"Oh!" she said.

"I'm surprised you never heard of Greenpeace," he said. He sounded nastier than he meant to sound.

"Well," she said. "I never did. But there are plenty of vegetarians in my school. One of my best friends is a vegetarian."

"You seem to be in a good mood."

"Oh, I am," she said. "I've had a wonderful

holiday. We had a delicious turkey—well—never mind about that. But the best part of the holiday is that my father isn't mad at me anymore."

Six people lined up at the desk. It took him a lot of time to get them books. Then a bunch of other people took their places.

Mrs. Douglas got her shot in about his being late. She said she would dock him fifteen minutes for the last time. Next time he was late, she said, she would start docking him half an hour.

He spent a couple of hours running back and forth between the stacks and the desk. Each time he came back, he looked for Tina and saw her reading her book.

At three o'clock, Mrs. Douglas told him to take his break. He could feel his heart thumping away as he stopped next to Tina's chair. He bent over her and whispered, "I'm going on a break now. We could sit in the park across the street and talk for fifteen minutes."

"Oh!" she said, looking up at him. Then she looked at her book.

"I'll put it behind the desk for you," he said. "It will be there when we get back."

"Okay," she said, standing up.

It was a warm, sunny day, and they sat on the grass. "I brought an apple," he said. "Do you want a piece?"

"Oh, yes," she said. "I like apples."

He cut her a piece with his penknife, and they both smiled at each other. Then he looked away and wondered what to say next.

"Do you make a lot of friends in the library?" she asked.

"Well—sometimes."

"I used to work in a service station," she said. "I made a lot of friends there."

She took a bite of her apple. She talked as she chewed. "That's where I first fell in love."

"Oh?" he said. "Who with?"

"Not with a person," she said. "With the Thunderbird. I mean, I always knew about Thunderbirds, but one day this guy came in with a 1956 Thunderbird. That year they still had the spare tire on the back, but I fell in love with it anyway. It was a bright red, and the upholstery was black. I just stood there, looking at it, my heart doing flip-flops. The guy said he had been working on it for a couple of years, and it ran like a dream. I asked him a lot of questions, and then he offered to take me for a ride."

"You went for a ride with a man you didn't know?"

"Oh, it was okay," Tina said. "You can tell a lot about a person by his car. I wouldn't trust anybody who drove around in a beat-up old Toyota or a banged-up little Chevy.

"Are you crazy?" Dennis said. "You never should take a ride with a strange man. Period."

Tina giggled. "You sound like my mother. Well, I guess I won't anymore. Especially now that I have my own Thunderbird. But I still think a person who takes good care of a Thunderbird has to be a pretty good person."

"That doesn't make any sense at all."

"Why not?" Tina said. "Look at you. I bet you would trust somebody who was good to animals. Wouldn't you?"

Dennis made a face. "I did," he said. "But I won't anymore."

"Oh?" Tina looked at him. She was waiting for him to go on.

"I mean it has nothing to do with the animals. I love animals, and I wouldn't ever trust somebody who was cruel to an animal. Last summer, I volunteered one day a week at the animal shelter. You should see the kinds of things people do to animals."

"I know," Tina said. "There's a kid next door who used to put a leash on his cat. He used to drag it along the street until its eyes almost popped out. I made him stop."

"That's nothing," Dennis said, "compared to the kinds of things you see at the animal shelter. There was a dog somebody kept in a basement for a whole year. He never took it out. It was only a year old, but it looked old and it was nearly blind. Then there was a cat with two broken legs because some weirdo dropped it out of a window. And a pigeon . . ."

"No," Tina said. "Don't tell me anymore."

Dennis shook his head. "If I were a judge, I'd sentence those people who hurt animals to the same kind of torture. I'd drop that weirdo out of the window, and I'd lock the other creep up in a basement."

"I don't think anybody should hurt animals," Tina said.

"People can protect themselves," Dennis said. "But an animal is helpless against a person."

"Anyway," Tina said, "what did you mean when you said you used to trust people who were good to animals but you wouldn't anymore?"

"Oh, I was thinking of Emily. I met her in the library last May. She was doing a report on harbor seals. She was great with animals. I really trusted her. She and I went around together all summer, and then she split up with me and picked up with Rick, my best friend. I mean, he used to be my best friend. I trusted him too. Maybe it's a mistake to trust people. Even people who are good with animals. He also belongs to Greenpeace. But we don't talk much anymore."

"You can really trust people who are good with Thunderbirds," Tina said. "I know because I belong to a Thunderbird club. The people are great. I mean, you can really trust them. You wouldn't find a greater bunch of people anywhere."

Dennis stood up. "I have to get back," he said. "My fifteen minutes are up."

"This was nice," Tina said as they walked back to the library. "I'm going to leave in an hour. My father started talking to me again on Thanksgiving. He promised to look at the engine with me when he gets back from his store."

A motorcycle whizzed by just a foot or two away from them as they crossed the street. Tina grabbed his arm. It felt good.

"Why is your father mad at you?"

34

She let go of his arm and smiled right into his face. Their eyes were about level. She was tall for a girl, and he was kind of short—around five feet eight.

"He's mad because I bought the Thunderbird. I told you he wanted me to save my money and buy one of those little foreign cars." She shuddered. "He figured I could get an old one, and we could work on it together."

"Is your father interested in cars?" Dennis asked.

"Uh-huh. He got me started. He and I always tune up his car, fix the brakes and change the plugs. We've put in alternators, starters and fuel pumps—easy things like that."

"Easy?"

"Oh, that's nothing. We've even done a valve job, and I know we wouldn't have any trouble rebuilding an engine. But when I came home with the Thunderbird . . ." She started giggling. "He didn't know I was going to buy it. I didn't tell him. I had it towed, and he was standing there when I brought it home. I was sitting in the tow truck, and my father just froze when it stopped and I got out. You should have seen his face! That was more than two weeks ago, and he just started talking to me again on Thanksgiving."

"You mean he didn't say anything at all then—when you brought the Thunderbird home?"

"Oh, sure. Then, he said plenty. He yelled so loud you could hear him around the corner. He said, 'You must be the dumbest girl in the whole world' and 'You won't get one red cent from me' and 'It's not going in the garage.' Things like that."

"Maybe he's right," Dennis said. "Maybe you should try to get rid of it."

"No! It's okay now. Thanksgiving he started talking to me. And later, he even looked inside the engine. He said for an old piece of junk, it really didn't look too bad. Then he helped me push it into the garage."

"Well," Dennis said, "I have to go back to work but . . ."

"He's coming home at four today, and if he'll help me, we can take out the engine and start working on it. But if he won't help me, I'm going to ask Roger to come over. He's that guy with the 1956 Thunderbird. He said he would help me. He's a great guy—the greatest guy I ever met, and you should see his Thunderbird. It's gorgeous!"

"I've got to go now," Dennis said.

He didn't say good-bye.

37

7

Friday
5:22 P.M.

"What happened to you? I've been looking for you since last Saturday."

"Oh, Tina!" Dennis said. "I've been working in the literature room. They had an emergency. Two kids quit, and some other people came down with the flu. So my boss sent me up there Monday and Wednesday nights."

"You're really early," she said. "How come you're so early?"

"I don't start until six," he said. "I'm doing some work for school."

She was holding the book on the Thunderbird.

"Aren't you finished with that book yet?" he asked her.

"Yes, I did finish it. But it makes me feel

38

good just looking at it. It's the only thing that makes me feel good lately."

He looked at the clock over the desk. He didn't have much time for his schoolwork.

"Are you very busy?" Tina asked. "Do you have time for a cup of coffee?"

"I don't drink coffee," he said.

"Or whatever you drink. I'll pay. We could go to the cafeteria across the street. I mean, if you have time."

"Is something wrong?" he asked.

"Everything is wrong." Her eyes filled up with tears.

"I drink herb teas," he said, "or juices. I drink juices too."

They walked across the street to the cafeteria. It was already dark out and windy.

"I hope I'm not taking you away from something important," she said.

"Monday," he told her, "I have to give a report on extinct birds."

"What does that mean?" she asked him.

"You don't know what 'extinct' means?" he said.

"I wouldn't ask you if I did, would I?" she snapped. "You really know how to make a person feel stupid."

"Okay, okay," he said. He knew that you

shouldn't hit a person when she was down, and Tina looked very down. " 'Extinct' means wiped out. Like the dinosaur and the saber-toothed tiger. They became extinct millions of years ago because the earth changed. But I'm doing my report on birds that became extinct because of man. Like the passenger pigeon. It was wiped out because of hunters. And the Carolina parakeet. It was wiped out because its feathers were used to make women's hats."

"That's very sad," Tina said.

"Yes, it is sad. And even today, lots of birds are endangered. Like the bald eagle and the whooping crane."

They walked into the cafeteria and stood on line, waiting for their drinks. Tina ordered a cup of black coffee. Dennis asked for peppermint tea, but they didn't have peppermint tea. He settled for a glass of orange juice. They sat down at a table in the rear.

"It really is sad," Tina said, "to think of all those animals dying out and never, never coming back again."

"Yes, it is."

"It's the same way with cars," she said. "Some of the most beautiful cars that have ever been built are no longer around. The cars they make

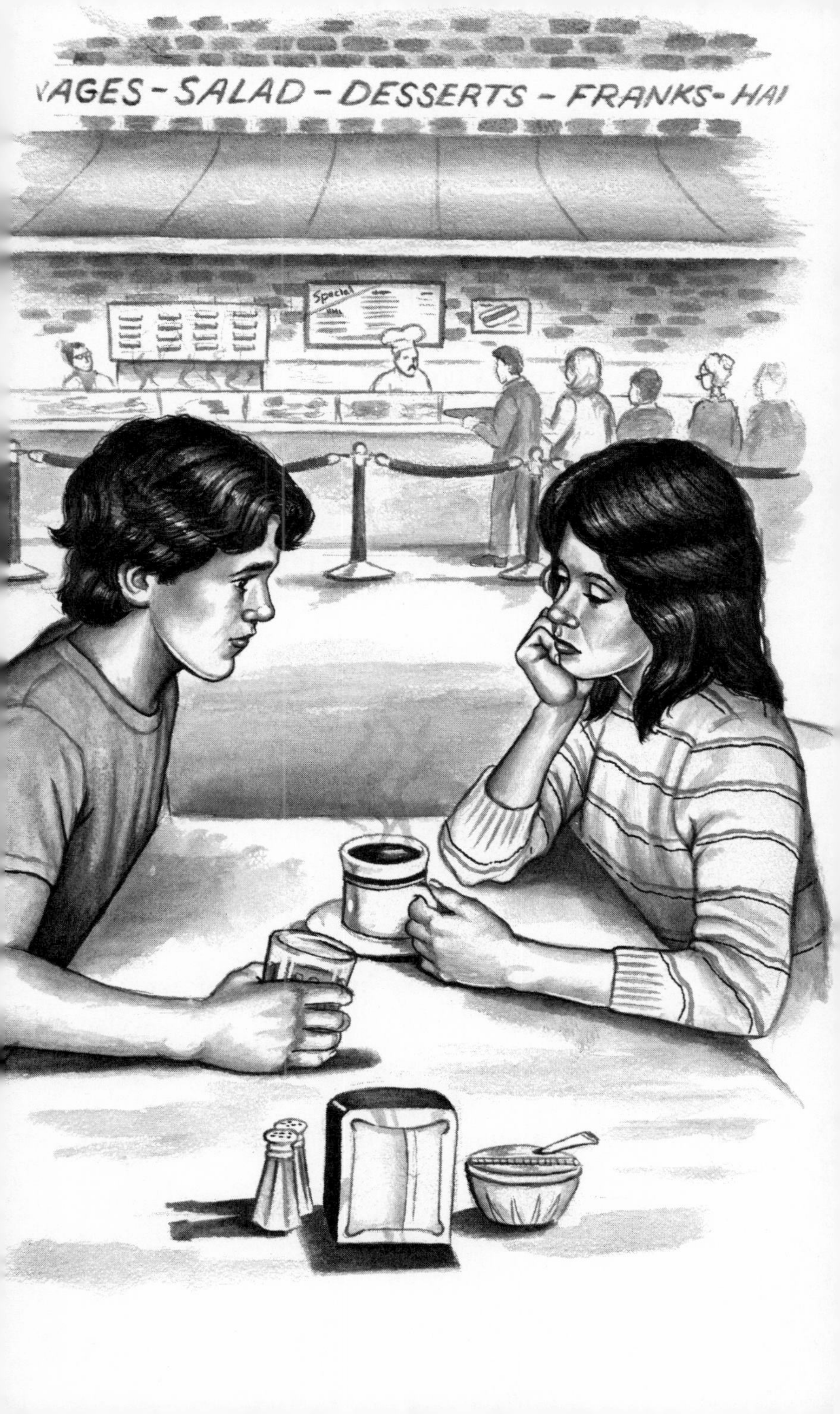

VAGES - SALAD - DESSERTS - FRANKS - HA
Special

nowadays . . ." Her face looked scornful. "They're just hunks of tin that rattle around when you drive in them. After 1960, the cars are like toys."

"It's not the same thing," Dennis muttered.

"I've had a terrible week," she said.

"Why? What happened? Last time I saw you, everything was going great. Even your father was coming around."

"Oh, yes. He's been okay," Tina said, taking a gulp of her coffee. "He worked with me on Saturday when he came back from the store and on Sunday too. He helped me take out the engine. He said it's going to need more than just a ring-and-valve job. The crankshaft and the main bearings will have to be replaced as well. Lots of other parts will have to be changed too. But he was impressed. He even got kind of excited. He said they don't make engines like that anymore."

"So? Isn't that what you wanted? What's wrong?"

"All those parts take money," she said. "I need a job, and I can't find one. The service station I used to work for closed down in September. Nobody else will hire me. They prefer boys. I tell them I had nearly a year's experience and I know more about cars than most guys. They don't believe me."

"Well, that's too bad," Dennis said, "but can't you get another kind of job?"

"I've been trying," she said. "I used to baby-sit for the Drexlers on Monday and Friday nights. But Mrs. Drexler's mother has moved to San Francisco, so she's going to baby-sit for them. There was a job in the bakery on Clement Street, but they wanted somebody who could come in at two. I'm in school until four. I'm willing to work nights and either Saturday or Sunday. I need one day free to work on my Thunderbird."

Dennis pushed his glass of orange juice away. It tasted flat. And sour. Why should he care if she found a job or not? But he did.

"They need a page up in the literature room," he said. "They need one right away. I bet they would hire you today."

"No kidding!" She began smiling but then she stopped. "What would I have to do? I mean, I don't know much about libraries. I hardly ever read books except for school."

"You don't have to know much about libraries to work as a page," he explained. "You have to put books away and get them out for people. You put the books on the shelf according to the author's last name if they're fiction. All you need to know is the alphabet. If it's non-fiction, it goes by number. As long as you can count, you can do that."

"I can count," she said, "but . . ." She looked down at her jeans and sweater. "I don't think I'm dressed right for a job interview."

"None of the pages dress up. Just go on up and ask for Mrs. Wong. Tell her you're a friend of mine and you just heard about the job. Tell her you can start immediately."

"Do you really think I have a chance?" she asked.

"Sure—they're desperate. They'll take any-body. Go right now. It's up on the second floor. The literature room. Ask for Mrs. Wong. Don't forget. And come down and tell me what hap-pens."

She jumped up and hurried out of the cafe-teria. He worked all night in the science room, but she never came back.

8

Saturday
3:25 P.M.

"There's a telephone call for you, Dennis," Mrs. Douglas said. She looked at the line of people waiting for books. "Please make it very short."

"Oh, hi, Dennis," Tina said, kind of breathlessly. "You know something? I didn't even know your name was Dennis. I just called and asked the librarian for you. I told her I wanted the boy who wears the dead-birds shirt, and she knew right away. . . ."

"I can't talk," he said. "It's very busy now."

"Okay, okay," she said, speaking very quickly. "I just wanted to say thanks. I got the job. I started working last night. That's why I couldn't come down and tell you. Oh, Dennis, it's just

great. I'll be working Tuesday, Thursday and
Friday nights and Sunday afternoons. I can work
on my car on Saturday and Sunday mornings
and . . ."

Mrs. Douglas was standing right over him
now.

"I've got to go," he said.

"Oh!" she said. "Well, I just wanted to say
thanks and . . ."

"I can't talk now," he said. "Good-bye!" And
he hung up.

9

"Hi, Tina. I just wanted to see how you were getting along."

"Oh, hello, Dennis."

"I needed a book for school," he lied.

"What book?" she asked.

"Oh, just any book. So I thought I'd stop by and see how you were doing."

"Pretty good," she said. She didn't look at him. She picked up a book and put it on the shelf. "They're very nice here. The other kids are friendly, and the brother of one of the librarians has a 1955 Thunderbird."

"Oh!"

She went on working, and there was a silence between them. He cleared his throat.

48

"Look, I'm sorry I couldn't talk to you on Saturday. Mrs. Douglas was really on my back."

"That's okay," she said, picking up another book and moving down the stack.

"I guess I should have called you back, but I didn't know your number."

"That's right," she said. "You didn't."

"I guess I must have sounded kind of rude."

"It's perfectly okay." She didn't look at him.

"Is Roger your boyfriend?" he asked.

"Roger?" She stopped shelving books and looked at him. "Of course he's not my boyfriend. He's twenty-eight years old. He's married. And he's got a kid."

"Here, let me help you," Dennis said. He picked up a couple of books and began shelving them.

"I was going to ask you if you wanted to get together," Tina said. "Maybe on a Friday night before work. Both of us work on Friday. I thought maybe we could have a hamburger at McDonald's—oh—well—or something else you can eat. I wanted to treat you because you helped me get the job. That's what I wanted to ask you over the phone but . . ."

She was standing next to him, looking at him and waiting.

"I have a lot of schoolwork to do in the library tonight," he said. "I could wait for you. Where do you live, anyway?"

"On Twenty-seventh Avenue—near Anza."

"Oh," he said, "that's great. I live on Clement near Fortieth. We could go home together."

"Yes," she said, "we could. And if you like, you can even come in and see the Thunderbird."

"Oh—the Thunderbird."

"I'd really like you to see it. I know you're not very interested in cars. . . ."

"No," he said. "I'm not very interested in cars."

"But I think when you see it, you'll change your mind. The design is so beautiful. Cars nowadays are ugly compared to my Thunderbird. I have a feeling you're going to be impressed."

"Uh, what school do you go to?" he asked.

"George Washington," she said. "Where do you go?"

"Lowell."

"Oh!"

"My parents wanted me to go to Lowell," he said quickly. "I really wanted to go to Washington. One of my best friends goes to Washington."

"What's his name?"

"Who?"

"Your friend who goes to Washington," she said.

"Bob. Bob Jennings."

"Oh, him!"

"Oh, do you know him?" he asked.

"Sure, I know him," she said. "He's in my French class, and last term he was in my civics class. He's the smartest kid in the school. I bet he gets A's in everything. He could have gone to Lowell."

"Well, see, that's what I mean," Dennis said. "Lots of smart kids go to Washington."

"Most of them go to Washington because they can't get into Lowell. I never could have gotten in. I didn't even try."

"There are lots of different ways to be smart," Dennis said quickly. "Marks are just one way."

"All I ever get are C's," Tina told him, "except in my shop classes. I get A's in my shop classes, especially in auto mechanics. Mr. Fine, my teacher, says I'm the best student he ever had."

"That's nice."

51

"I bet you get all A's," she said.

"Not always," he told her. "Not in shop. I mean, they don't have shop classes in Lowell, but in junior high I always got C's in shop."

"No kidding?" She was smiling at him now, and he stopped shelving to smile back at her. Right into her face.

10

Friday
5:15 P.M.

"This was a good idea," Tina said, unwrapping her sandwich.

"Well, now that you're working for the library, we can both eat in the staff lounge."

Dennis unwrapped his sandwich. He could smell her sandwich before he even saw it—salami. It was a big sandwich on a huge French roll. She had potato chips too and a can of Coke.

"What kind of sandwich do you have?" Tina asked.

"Vegetables and tofu in pita bread."

"What's that?"

"Here—do you want a bite?"

She hesitated and then took a little nibble.

He watched her and waited as she slowly chewed and swallowed.

"Well," she said finally, "it's—it's—interesting."

"Do you want another bite?" he offered.

"No, no, thank you. Do you want a bite of my sandwich?"

"No, thank you."

"Oh, that's right. I keep forgetting. You're a vegetarian. When did you stop eating meat?"

"A few years ago."

She took a big bite of her sandwich. "It must be very hard."

"No, it isn't," he said, trying not to look at her mouth full of salami. "I feel much better since I stopped."

"I'd feel horrible if I couldn't eat hamburgers or pepperoni pizzas or bacon," she said.

He decided to change the subject. "What are you doing for Christmas?"

"I can hardly wait," she said. "I got my parents to agree to give me money instead of presents. I'm telling everybody to give me money. I'll have my first paycheck from the library by then, so I can start buying parts. Dad will have some days off, and he said he'd work with me."

She smiled. Some salami and bread pieces

55

were stuck in her teeth. "He's really getting excited about my Thunderbird. Did you notice how he kept going on and on when he met you on Tuesday? Even I'm not that bad."

"Yes," Dennis said, "I did notice."

"And wasn't it funny how he thought you were really crazy about cars too. I told him you weren't, but he didn't believe me."

"He seems very . . . very nice."

"Oh, he's a great guy. And he liked you too. He said he thought you were very intelligent."

"We didn't really talk much."

"I know. He went on and on about the Thunderbird. But you'll see. He's interested in lots of things."

"Like what?"

"Oh—well—politics. And sewers. He thinks the sewers in this city are a disgrace. He keeps writing letters to the mayor. On our street, the sewers back up every time it rains. Maybe he'll tell you about it next time you're over."

"I liked your dog," Dennis said. "He's a beagle, isn't he?"

"Uh-huh. But Dennis, you didn't tell me what you thought of my Thunderbird."

"I thought I did."

"No, you didn't."

"Well, it's . . . it's kind of banged up, isn't it?"

"Sure it is. But just you wait until we fix it up. I'm so happy my father is going to help me. He knows so much about cars. He wanted to be an automobile mechanic too, but he always had to help out in his father's store."

"Do you really want to be an automobile mechanic?"

Tina nodded and took another bite out of her sandwich.

"But it's such dirty work," Dennis told her. "And you breathe gasoline fumes all day. It's bad for your health too."

"I don't want to work on just any cars," she said. "I want to restore old sports cars like Thunderbirds and maybe Porsches and Jaguars. I want to make them really go. I want to see them smoking down roads . . ."

"Polluting the air," Dennis said before he could help himself.

But she didn't hear him. She had a dreamy, faraway look in her eyes.

"Anyway," he said, "I was thinking—tonight after work, we could go to a movie. There's one playing at the Regency—the new Woody Allen movie. It starts at nine thirty, so we shouldn't have any trouble getting there on time."

"I don't like him." Tina made a face.

"Who?"

"Woody Allen," she said. "I think he's stupid."

"Well, we could go to some other movie then," he said. "Whatever you say."

Tina shook her head. "I can't because I'm saving my money for the Thunderbird."

"Oh!"

"But you know what? Why don't you just come over to my house after work?"

"I don't know," he said. "I thought it would be nice to go out somewhere."

"I'd rather talk," she said, "so why don't you just come over to my house. It will give us a chance to talk. There are a lot of things I'd like to know about you."

"Like what?"

"Like what you're interested in. What you want to do when you get out of high school."

"I want to be a vet," he said.

"You really love animals, don't you?"

"Yes, I do. My father thinks I should go to medical school."

"What does your father do?" Tina asked.

"He's a doctor. So is my mother. My family is kind of boring that way. I have an older sister who's in medical school too."

"I don't think that's boring," Tina said.

Dennis looked down at the table. He looked at her hand, lying there. Then he looked around the room. There were several other people in the room.

"I hate to think of animals suffering," Dennis said. "If I could do something—a little—to help, I wouldn't feel so bad."

"You're a very kind person," Tina said.

"No, I'm not." Dennis kept looking at her hand. "I have a bad temper. My father says the reason I want to be a vet is because I get along better with animals than with people."

"I think you're a kind person," Tina said. "You can be kind even if you have a bad temper. I think you're smart too. I knew it the first time you opened your mouth. Even though you were so mean, I knew you were smart."

"I had no right talking to you that way," Dennis said. "I feel bad whenever I think of it."

"I laugh when I think of it," said Tina. "We really got off to a terrible start. I never went out with anybody before who started out by insulting me."

"Have you gone out with a lot of different guys?"

"Well—a few. My mother wouldn't let me go

out alone with a boy until I was fifteen. I could have, but she said no."

"I'm sure you could have," he said. "You're such a pretty girl."

Her cheeks turned almost red. "No, I'm not," she said.

"Yes, you are." He moved his hand closer to hers, and she reached out and took it. There were people in the room, but she didn't care.

"Well, you're pretty cute yourself," she said.

"My eyes are too small, and my ears are too big, and I'm only five feet eight."

"Tell me about your old girlfriends." She put down her sandwich.

"I asked you first about your boyfriends."

"You tell me first."

"There isn't much to tell." He couldn't eat his sandwich. You needed two hands to hold a pita sandwich. And she still had her hand over his. But he didn't mind. "There was Emily last summer. I told you about her. And when I was a junior . . ."

"Oh? You're a senior now?"

"Yes. What about you?"

"I'm a senior too." She beamed at him.

"So when I was a junior," he continued, "I met a girl in my anti-nuke group. Her name

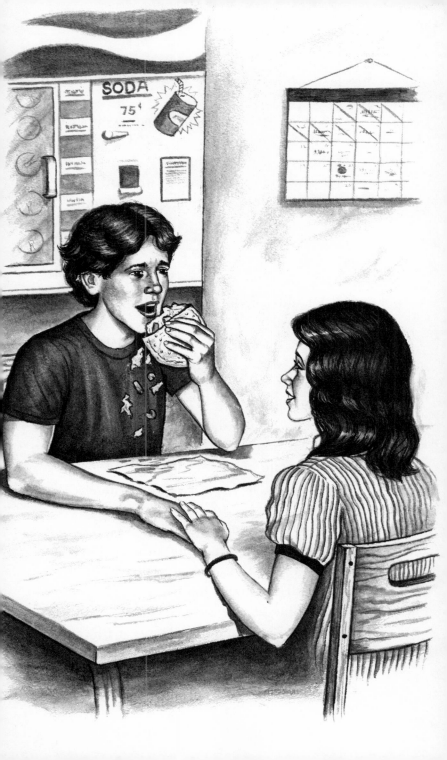

was Sara. She was—she is a nice girl. Smart too."

"I guess all your girlfriends have been smart," Tina said. She took away her hand.

"Well, yes," he admitted.

"Marks aren't everything," Tina said.

"Well, no. I told you that the other day," he said quickly.

"People can be smart in lots of different ways," Tina said.

"That's right."

She let out a long breath. "Well, what happened to Sara?"

"Oh—she moved. To South Dakota. We wrote for a while, but then it kind of petered out."

"I'm glad she moved," Tina said, opening her bag of potato chips. She held it out to him. He took one and chewed it carefully. Ordinarily he never ate potato chips.

"Well, that's it for me—pretty much," he said. "What about you?"

"Elliot Dean," she said. "He was the only one. I went out with some others, but they didn't really count."

"Well, tell me about him."

"I met him at the service station. He was driving a 1973 Plymouth Duster with a V-8 engine. He asked me to go out with him as soon as I checked his oil."

"You went out with him right away?"

"Certainly not," Tina said. "I would never go out with somebody who drives a Duster. At least, not the first time he asked me. It was in good shape, though. He came back a few times, and it turned out he was a friend of my cousin. So I started going out with him. He knew a lot about cars, and that Duster of his could really go. Sometimes we could do ninety on an empty road."

"You went ninety miles an hour," he said.

"Well, he tried to get it up to a hundred, but it began to make funny noises. I told him to stop."

"You could have been killed, Tina, going that fast. It's against the law too. You could have been arrested."

"No, not me," she said. "I wasn't the one who was driving. I didn't have my license yet."

Dennis picked up his sandwich and bit off a big piece. Some of the vegetables fell out onto his waxed bag.

She looked off into space. "We had a good time," she said, "as long as the car was moving. But it got to be a problem whenever he stopped. Maybe he was just too old for me.

That was last year. I wasn't sixteen yet, and he was nineteen."

"What about your parents?" Dennis asked. "How come they let you go out with him?"

"Well, he was a friend of my cousin. And he was always very polite with my parents. He even brought my mother flowers. And he had a good job managing a fruit and vegetable store. They thought he was a great guy. They didn't know what he kept trying to do to me in the backseat of his Duster."

"Did they know he drove ninety miles an hour with you? Did you tell them that?"

"They didn't ask me how fast he drove. But I decided he was getting too hard for me to handle, so I broke up with him. I thought I would miss him more. We once drove down to Santa Cruz in less than an hour. But I didn't miss him after the first couple of weeks. And that Duster didn't really have any class."

"Well, I don't drive," Dennis said. "I don't have a license, and maybe I'll never get one. So if you're going to go around with me, it will have to be on foot or on city buses."

"That's all right. In a few months, maybe, my Thunderbird will be ready to go. I can wait until then."

"So can I," said Dennis.

64

11

Saturday
1:12 P.M.

"I think you're getting worse and worse, Dennis," said Mrs. Douglas. "If you can't change, maybe you had better look for another job."

"That's all right with me, Mrs. Douglas," Dennis said. "I didn't get out of here last night until 9:18. If you don't believe me, you can just look at my time card."

He was wearing his dead-birds tee shirt—the one that said STOP TOXIC WASTE. It was supposed to be a tan shirt with blue birds and letters, but he had thrown different colored clothes together last time he did the laundry. The shirt looked a crazy mud-pink color with purple birds and letters. It had also shrunk in the wash.

"I've already told you, Dennis, that it's not the same thing."

"Well, I don't think it's fair," Dennis told her.

"You're the one who's not being fair," she said. "Everybody else manages to get to work on time. You're the only one. We can't have a special rule just for you. You're just going to have to get here on time."

"I'm quitting, Mrs. Douglas," he said. "I'll work next week up through Friday, but then I'm quitting. You'll have to find somebody else to pick on."

12

"Someone said you were back here in the stacks, shelving books."

"Oh—yeah—hello, Tina," Dennis said. He picked up a couple of books and put them on the shelf.

"I came in at six o'clock and waited for you, but I guess you got here early." She laughed. "You must be turning over a new leaf."

A lot of good it was going to do, he thought. He had come in early—at 5:48 actually, but Mrs. Douglas was still out sick. She had been sick all week. Today would be his last day at the library.

"This is my last day," he said angrily, shoving a book up on the shelf.

"Your last day?"

"Yeah—my last day. I quit."

"But why?" she wanted to know.

"I got sick of it," he said. "Sick of all the work and Mrs. Douglas picking on me for everything. I work harder than any of the other pages, but she's never satisfied."

"Oh, Dennis," Tina said, "that's terrible. Won't she change her mind?"

"I'm the one who quit," he said. "I'm not going to change my mind. And anyway, she's been out sick all week."

She didn't say anything, and he moved the truck a little further along. He kept shelving the books without looking at her. Finally, she asked, "What will you do?"

"I don't know," he said.

"Will you look for another job?"

"Well, sure," he said, "but they're not so easy to find. You should know that."

"Yes," she said, "I do know it. If it wasn't for you, I'd probably still be looking. Which is why I feel so bad for you. But Dennis, couldn't you make up with Mrs. Douglas? You could call her at home. You could apologize over the phone."

"For what?" he said. "You don't even know

69

what happened, but you're saying I should apologize. How do you know it wasn't her fault?"

He stopped putting away the books and turned to face her. She had a worried wrinkle across her forehead as she looked back at him. "I guess I figured it was because you were late. She was always mad at you for that."

"Well, plenty of times I stayed later than nine o'clock," he said. "But she never said anything about that."

"Oh, Dennis," Tina said, moving over to him and putting a hand on his arm. "I'm so sorry. I know how much you liked this job."

He felt like crying. Because she was right. He did like the job. And he knew he had goofed.

"No," he lied, moving away from her hand. "I was getting sick of it. You'll see. It gets pretty boring after a while."

"I just wish I could find a job for you," Tina said. "I owe you one."

"Fixing the Thunderbird, maybe?" he said. "No, thanks."

As soon as he said it, he was sorry. He wanted to tell her he was sorry, but he didn't. He just kept on shelving books and not looking at her.

"Drop dead, Dennis!" she said.

He could hear her footsteps as she walked away. He looked up, watching her move quickly away from him, down the narrow aisle. He kept watching her back, but then, suddenly, she slowed down, hesitated and turned. He dropped his eyes again to the books on his truck. He could hear her steps returning. He picked up a book and put it on the shelf.

"Dennis," Tina said, moving up very close to him. "You really are a jerk. Do you know that?"

He shrugged his shoulders and picked out another book.

"You're jealous of my car, Dennis," Tina said. "I just realized it."

"I'm not jealous!"

"Yes, you are." She shook her head. "And you're a jerk because . . . well, because we were having a pretty good time last Friday, going home after work. On the number 5 bus. I was having a good time anyway, and I thought you were too."

Dennis remembered how they held hands on the bus. They had talked about school and their old boyfriends and girlfriends. They had laughed a lot. Once she had put her head down on his shoulder.

72

"I was," he said. "And I thought it was going to be the beginning of something big. But everything changed as soon as we got to your house."

"Nothing changed."

"Yes, it did," he said angrily. "I realized something about you. You're a different person around that dumb, ugly car."

"My Thunderbird!"

"Yes, your Thunderbird. You're a real Dr. Jekyll and Mr. Hyde. That car is like some kind of evil spirit. It casts a spell over you. As soon as you go near it, you change."

"I don't change. Just because the repair manual came in the mail, and I had to show a couple of things to my father."

"You could have shown it to him later. After I left. But no. You went on and on, squealing like a little pig over it. You kept oohing and aahing over every page. You kept showing me diagrams that I wasn't interested in and telling me what kind of parts you needed. You didn't even notice how bored I was. You never thought of me for a minute."

"Okay, okay," she said. "So I was wrong. I'm sorry."

"And then Roger called, and you said you

would talk to him for just a few minutes. But you didn't. You must have been on the phone twenty minutes. Can you blame me for getting sore?"

"I said I was sorry."

"I'm sorry too," he said, "because I realized that it was hopeless. I realized you've got an obsession. All you're interested in is your Thunderbird. You haven't got time for anything or anybody else. All you care about is your Thunderbird."

She was looking at his shirt—the No Nukes shirt. She pointed her finger at it and said, "But if I had an obsession about Greenwood or that anti-nuke group of yours, it would be different, right?"

"Greenpeace," he said, "not Greenwood. And yes, it would be different because you would be doing something good. Something important. Something that mattered."

"Something that mattered?" she said. "But I am doing something that matters. Something important. Like you want to rescue those extinct animals. I'm doing the same thing. I'm taking an old, beat-up, neglected car that nobody wanted. And I'm going to bring it back to life again. I'm going to make it go. I'm not going to hurt anybody or kill any animals. I'm going to bring an old car back to life. I'm doing something good."

"You go speeding down the freeway at ninety miles an hour," Dennis said. "You call that good?"

"No," she said, looking him straight in the eye. "That's not good, and I guess I better change. Lots of things I don't do right, and I'm sorry for and try to change. I'm sorry for what happened last Friday night. I'll try not to let it happen again. But Dennis, I'm not perfect. Are you?"

"No," Dennis said. "I'm not."

"See! Nobody is."

"I try to do good things," he said. "I want to make the world a better place. For everybody. People as well as animals."

"That's hard," she said. "No wonder you get so grouchy."

"I'm good with animals," he told her. "Dogs always come up to me and lick my hands. Even cats jump into my lap. They know who their friends are. It's different with people."

"I wouldn't want people licking my hands or jumping into my lap." She was grinning at him. He looked away and tried not to smile.

"No," he said, "I'm not perfect. I have trouble getting along with people. I don't know why."

"Maybe you expect too much," she told him. "Everybody can't change the world. Some people just want to have fun. Maybe you need to have a little more fun in your life."

He didn't say anything. After a while, she said, "You know, Dennis, it's going to seem very funny working here in the library without you. But, in a way, I'm glad you quit."

"Why?" he asked.

"Because it was kind of hopeless. You worked Mondays, Wednesdays, Fridays and half-day Saturdays. I worked Tuesdays, Thursdays, Fridays and half-day Sundays. That left us only half days on Saturdays and Sundays."

"No," he said, "not Saturdays and Sundays. You'd be working on your Thunderbird on Saturdays and Sundays."

"That's right," she said, looking straight at him. "Lots of times I will—until I get it going."

He shrugged his shoulders, dropped his eyes and started shelving books again.

"Friends have to share," she said. "I'd be willing to share you with the things you like to do. Even if I don't want to do them. Why can't you do the same with me?"

He kept shelving his books, but he asked her, "Would you ever come with me to a Greenpeace meeting?"

"Why, sure," she said, "as long as you come with me to my Thunderbird club."

He burst out laughing.

"There," she said. "That's better."

"But what will we have to talk about?"

"Lots of things," she said. "We disagree on just about everything. It should give us lots to talk about—all the things we don't agree on."

"You know something, Tina," he said. "I'm sorry for being so mean. Lots of times I'm sorry when I say mean things, but then I can't say so. I have a bad temper. I guess you already know that."

"Oh, I do. I do," she said.

"So why . . ."

"Why do I like you?"

"Uh-huh."

"Maybe because you remind me of my Thunderbird. You could use a complete overhauling if you're ever going to run properly. You've got a lot of possibilities, and your chassis is pretty solid, but you do have some wires loose, and your radiator keeps overheating . . ."

He didn't let her finish.

"Watch out!" she yelled as he reached for her over the book truck. "You're knocking over those books."

But he didn't care. For the next few minutes, he didn't care about anything. Not even her Thunderbird.